Ex Líbris

Nathan Wada

# Sleeping Over

## BARBARA LUCAS

## pictures by Stella Ormai

Macmillan Publishing Company   New York

"Goodnight, Froggie," said
Bitty Bear.

"Goodnight," said Froggie Green.

"Spending the night at your house
is fun."

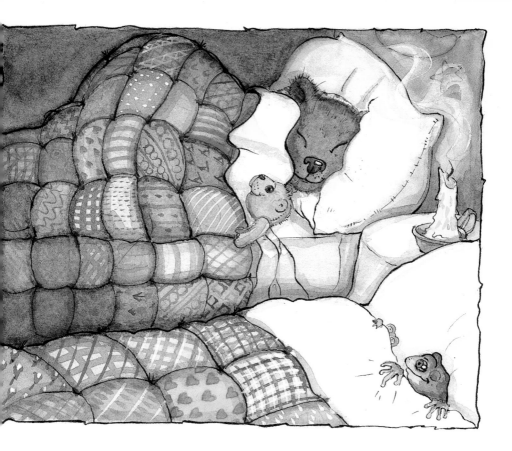

Bitty Bear fell fast asleep.

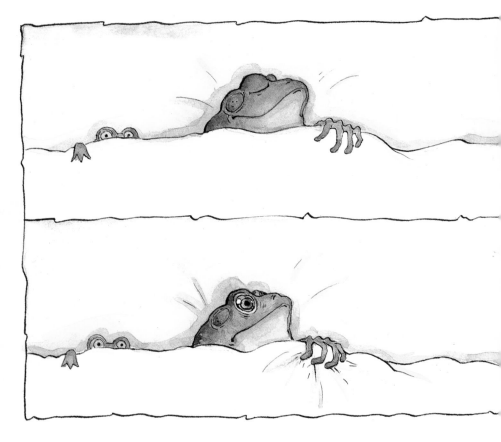

Froggie shut his eyes, then
opened them again.

"This bed feels very strange,"
he said.

"I will sleep on the floor."

The floor was very hard.

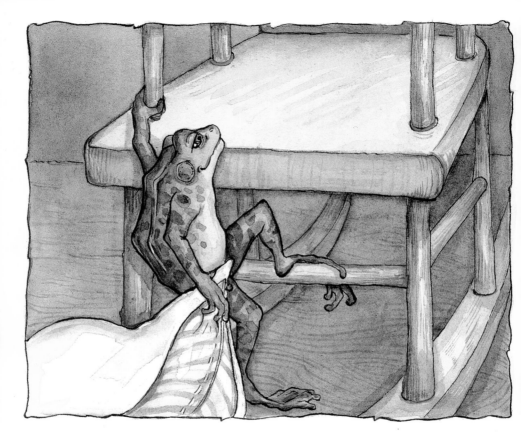

"I will sleep on the chair."

The chair rocked back and forth.

*Drip. Drip. Drip. Drip.*

Froggie heard a wonderful sound.

Just listening made his skin
feel good.

"Ah..." said Froggie.
"Just like my bed at home."

For Jo – B.L.
For Richard – S.O.

LUCAS EVANS BOOKS

Macmillan Publishing Company, 866 Third Avenue, New York, NY 10022
Collier Macmillan Canada, Inc.

Printed and bound in Japan
First American Edition

10 9 8 7 6 5 4 3 2 1

The text of this book is set in 18 pt. Bembo. The illustrations are rendered in watercolor and ink.

Library of Congress Cataloging-in-Publication Data
Lucas, Barbara. Sleeping over.
Summary: While spending the night at Bitty Bear's house, Froggie Green feels uncomfortable until he hears the familiar sound of dripping water. [1. Sleep – Fiction. 2. Frogs – Fiction] I. Ormai, Stella, ill. II. Title. PZ7.L9686S1 1986 [E] 85-23649
ISBN 0-02-761360-7 ISBN 0-02-759590-0 (pbk.)